W9-BCR-680

The Magic Horse

Retold and Illustrated by

SALLY SCOTT

GREENWILLOW BOOKS NEW YORK

FOR MY MOTHER

First published in Great Britain in 1985 by Julia MacRae Books

Printed in Belgium
First American Edition 10 9 8 7 6 5 4 3 2 1

This text has been retold and adapted from "The Ebony Horse,"
a story from *The Arabian Nights* translated by Sir Richard Burton

Library of Congress Cataloging in Publication Data
Scott, Sally. The magic horse.
Summary: In order to marry the beautiful princess that he loves, a Persian
prince must outwit an evil magician and use the magic horse to his advantage.
1. Children's stories, American. [1. Fairy tales. 2. Princes—Fiction]
I. Title. PZ8.S316Mag 1985 [E] 85-5449
ISBN 0-688-05897-3 ISBN 0-688-05898-1 (lib. bdg.)

LONG AGO in Persia there lived a rich and powerful King, who had one son and one daughter. Twice a year he held a festival, when his people came to him with gifts and greetings.

On one such day, a Wizard approached and showed the King a horse carved from the blackest ebony, inlaid with gold and jewels. It was so beautifully made, is seemed almost alive.

"Sire," said the Wizard, "this is a very special horse—a magic horse. Whoever mounts it may travel anywhere he chooses and in no time at all."

The King was delighted and asked the Wizard to demonstrate the horse's powers. The Wizard mounted the horse and turned a peg behind its ear. At once, horse and rider soared up into the air, flying higher and higher into the sky above the Palace.

The King was amazed. "By Allah!" he cried, when the Wizard returned, "ask what you will for this magic horse, and it is yours."

"Sire," said the Wizard, "I ask for your daughter's hand in marriage."

All who heard this laughed heartily. The Wizard was old and ugly, and the Princess was as young and beautiful as the crescent moon.

The Princess was horrified at the very thought of such a match, and asked her brother, Prince Kamar al-Akmar, to help her. The Prince went at once to the King.

"It is an insolent demand, my father! I am sure you will not agree."

"Indeed, indeed, my son," sighed the King. "And after all the Wizard may be satisfied with gold instead. But take a look at this horse—by Allah, it is a wonderful thing."

When he saw the magic horse, Prince Kamar al-Akmar was so impressed that he leapt into the saddle at once.

The Wizard was furious at the Prince's interference. He stepped forward and pointing to a peg behind the horse's ear, he said, "Turn this, O Prince."

As soon as the Prince did so, the horse began to move. It rose into the air, up and up, higher and higher, until Prince Kamar al-Akmar was carried out of sight.

The King ordered the Wizard to make the magic horse descend.

"I cannot, Sire," replied the Wizard. "Everything happened so quickly I had no time to show the Prince how to bring the horse down."

The King flew into a rage. He had the Wizard thrown into prison and then, believing he had lost his only son, he ordered the Palace to go into mourning.

The Prince meanwhile had begun to be alarmed. When he turned the peg that the Wizard had shown him, the horse only rose higher. Quickly he searched, and to his relief he found a second peg behind the horse's other ear. In no time at all he learned to make the horse go higher or lower, faster or slower at a touch.

"Allah be praised!" he cried, and turned his attention to the scene below him. He marvelled at the countries he was passing over, the mountains and seas and cities and plains, until he realised that the day was rapidly drawing to a close.

Below him was a beautiful city, whose domes and towers and minarets shone like gold in the evening sun. He decided to rest there for the night, before returning home in the morning.

In the middle of the city was a great white marble palace, and he set the horse down on its roof. The Prince was very hungry and thirsty but he dared not leave the horse until late at night when all the inhabitants would be asleep.

At midnight, he went down a staircase and found himself in a magnificent court, paved with marble. He saw a light shimmering through a half-closed door, and making his way towards it, he stepped inside.

A guard lay sleeping by the glow of a lamp, his sabre at his side. Prince Kamar al-Akmar crept silently across the room and, raising the curtain to an inner chamber, he looked inside.

In the middle of the room was a jewelled couch, and on it, fast asleep, lay the most beautiful princess in the world.

The Prince was enchanted. He moved softly forward and kissed her on the cheek. At once she stirred, opened her eyes and looked with wonder at the handsome Prince. There and then she fell in love with him, and he with her.

The Princess knew it was dangerous for the Prince to remain in her chamber. She said he must leave at once, but begged to go with him. The Prince joyfully agreed.

They crept out onto the roof and mounted the magic horse, setting off just as dawn began to break over the marble palace.

They flew over lands and seas and mountains until at last they came to the Prince's homeland. He set down the horse in a summer pavilion just outside the walls of the city.

"Wait here, my love, while I go and greet my father," the Prince said. "I will prepare him, so that you may be received as befits your royal rank."

The Prince hastened to the Palace and at sight of him there was great rejoicing. The King welcomed him with tears in his eyes and, on hearing of the Princess, declared that he would be delighted to receive her. A royal litter was prepared, with a procession of guards and slaves to bring her into the city with all due ceremony.

The King now sent word to the dungeons that the Wizard should be released, since the Prince had returned safely after all.

But the Wizard, who was furious at his imprisonment, was determined to be revenged. When he learned of the coming marriage and the whereabouts of the Princess, he hurried to reach the summer pavilion before the procession arrived.

"My lady," said the Wizard, "I have been sent by my master, Prince Kamar al-Akmar, to bring you into the city. It is his wish that you enter it upon the wonderful horse which brought you here."

"As the Prince desires," replied the Princess, and she and the Wizard mounted the magic horse.

They were soaring high over the city as Prince Kamar al-Akmar arrived with the procession. He heard a mocking laugh far above him, and looking up saw the Wizard and the Princess on the magic horse, just disappearing from sight.

The Prince was in despair. He returned to the city, and would see no one in his grief.

Days passed, until one morning the Prince dried his tears and resolved to find the Princess, even if it should take him the rest of his life. He dressed in simple travelling clothes, and taking a purse full of money, set out on his search.

Meanwhile the Princess soon realised that she had been tricked, and she implored the Wizard to take her back to her Prince. But her entreaties were in vain. All day and all night they travelled, until at last the horse alighted in a strange land, in a clearing in the middle of a wood.

The Princess cried out for help. As luck would have it, the Sultan of that land was out hunting, and heard her screams.

Hastening to the spot, he was amazed to see the beautiful girl struggling in the arms of the old Wizard.

"By Allah, free that lady!" he ordered.

"She is my wife," replied the Wizard, "and I shall do as I please!"

"As Allah is merciful, I am not his wife," cried the Princess. "He is a wicked man, and a magician, who has stolen me away!"

The Sultan had no need to hear more. He ordered his men to seize the Wizard and throw him into prison. Then he took the Princess and the magic horse back to his palace. But the Princess's relief was short-lived, for the Sultan, too, was enchanted by her beauty and resolved to marry her himself.

The Princess was alarmed, and so she decided to gain time by pretending to be mad. She tore her clothes and her hair, shrieked, and rolled on the floor, and attacked the Sultan whenever he tried to approach her.

He sent his physicians to examine the girl, but she would not let them near her, and so they declared her case to be hopeless. The Sultan offered a large reward to anyone who could cure the Princess.

All this time, the Prince had been wandering from country to country, asking for news of an ebony flying horse and a beautiful Princess. But no-one had seen or heard of them.

One day he came to the land of the Sultan, and there he learned of the mad Princess and the search for anyone who could cure her. At once, he disguised himself as a physician and went to the Palace.

The Sultan ordered that he be shown to the Princess's chamber, where he could observe her from behind a lattice, since she would allow no-one to come near her.

There sat his Princess, beautiful and distraught, weeping, and singing a melancholy song.

He returned to the Sultan and said that he knew both the nature of her illness and the cure.

"But, Sire, in order to deal properly with the case, I must know how the Princess came here," said the Prince.

The Sultan told him how he had rescued the Princess and the ebony horse.

"Ah," said the Prince, nodding wisely, "it would seem that this horse has much to do with the condition of the Princess. Tell me, Sire, is it still in your possession?"

"Yes indeed," said the Sultan. The Prince told him to keep the horse in readiness, for he would have need of it during the treatment.

Then he returned to the Princess's chamber. Thinking he was another physician, she began to shout and shake her fist at him, until he spoke to her. "Do you not know me?" he said.

The Princess at once recognised the voice of her Prince, and was overjoyed. Then he told her of his plan.

"And you, my love," he said, "must now receive the Sultan happily, so that he believes I have cured you, and will trust me."

Later, when the Sultan came to her she received him with charm and courtesy. He was delighted and promised to reward the physician.

"And now, Allah be praised, the marriage can take place without delay," he cried.

"Ah, Sire," said the Prince, "I must advise against being too hasty in this matter. In order to effect a complete cure, the magic must be cast out of the horse, otherwise I fear the madness will return to the Princess."

The Sultan, willing to do anything which would avoid such a catastrophe, agreed at once.

"The horse," said the Prince, "must be brought to the spot where it first landed, together with the Princess and such items as I require, and there I shall proceed with the treatment."

"Of course, of course! By Allah, it shall be as you wish, O most excellent physician!" the Sultan exclaimed.

According to the Prince's orders, the Princess was arrayed in wedding finery, and she and the magic horse were taken to the clearing in the wood. At the Prince's command, she was lifted onto the horse, while he turned to the courtiers.

"On no account," he cried, "must anyone approach the horse during the ceremony. No doubt you will see it buck and start, but any interference will ruin my work and will do untold damage to the Princess." Then turning to the Sultan, he bowed. "With your leave, Sire?"

"Proceed, proceed!" cried the Sultan, eagerly.

The Prince took a taper and lit the charcoal burners and the incense which had been set in a circle round the horse. Then he began to pace around it, muttering strange words and incantations, while the courtiers looked on expectantly.

Soon the incense began to give off great clouds of perfumed smoke. The Prince leapt onto the magic horse behind the Princess, turned the peg, and the next moment horse and riders rose up into the sky. They soared high above the heads of the Sultan and his men, before disappearing from their view.

Half the day the Sultan waited for their return, until at last he realised that he had been tricked.

The Prince and the Princess returned to the Prince's homeland. An Ambassador was sent to ask her father's consent to the marriage. He was delighted to agree, thankful that she was safe and well. And so Prince Kamar al-Akmar and his Princess were married without more ado, with much feasting and rejoicing.

But the King ordered that the magic horse be broken up into a thousand pieces so that it would never fly again.